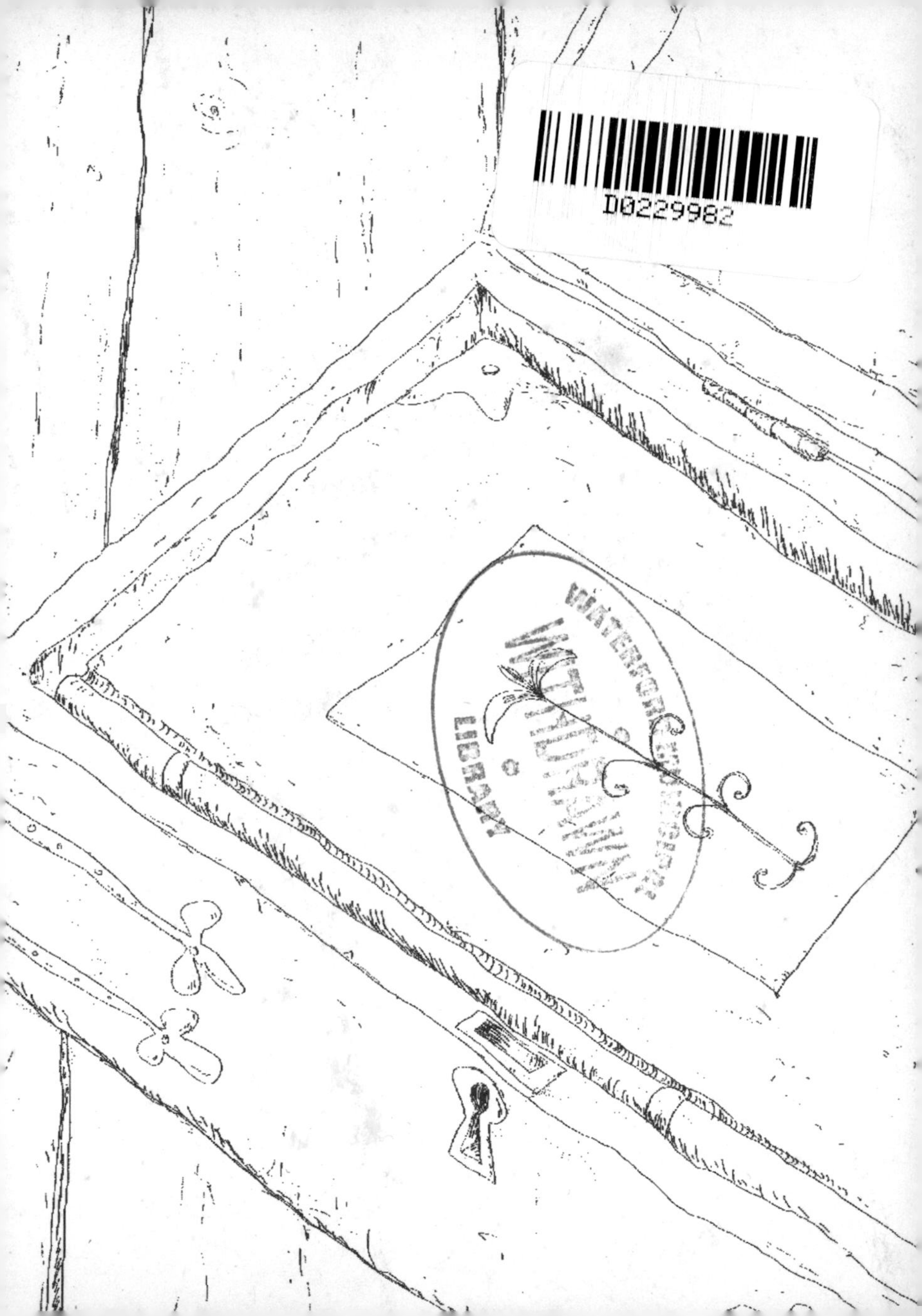

JOE O'BRIEN is an award-winning gardener who lives in Ballyfermot in Dublin. This is his seventh book about the wonderful world of Alfie Green.

DEDICATION

The *Alfie Green* series is dedicated to my son, Ethan, who in his short time in this world taught me to be strong, happy and thankful for the gift of life. Thank you, Ethan, for the inspiration to write.

Alfie Green and the Supersonic Subway is dedicated to David, Noreen, Daniel and Niamh, down under. Wouldn't it be wonderful if Alfie's Supersonic Subway went all the way to Australia!

ACKNOWLEDGEMENTS:
A big thank you to all at The O'Brien Press, to Jean Texier, and, of course, to my readers.

* * *

JEAN TEXIER is a storyboard artist and illustrator. Initially trained in animation, he has worked in the film industry for many years.

ALFIE GREEN AND THE SUPERSONIC SUBWAY

Joe O'Brien
Illustrated by Jean Texier

THE O'BRIEN PRESS
DUBLIN

First published 2008 by The O'Brien Press Ltd.,
12 Terenure Road East, Rathgar, Dublin 6, Ireland.
Tel: +353 1 4923333; Fax: +353 1 4922777
E-mail: books@obrien.ie
Website: www.obrien.ie

ISBN: 978-1-84717-095-8

British Library Cataloguing-in-Publication Data
O'Brien, Joe
Alfie Green and the supersonic subway

1. Green, Alfie (Fictitious character) - Juvenile fiction
2. Magic - Juvenile fiction 3.Children's stories
I. Title II. Texier, Jean
823.9'2[J]

1 2 3 4 5 6 7 8 9 10
08 09 10 11

The O'Brien Press receives
assistance from

Editing, typesetting, layout, design: The O'Brien Press Ltd.
Illustrations: Jean Texier
Printed and bound by ScandBook AB, Sweden.

CONTENTS

CHAPTER 1

A HEAP OF JUNK

Fitzer and Alfie were working hard to get their go-kart ready for the Budsville go-kart races. They tightened nuts, straightened wheels and greased axles. But The Green Machine still didn't look as good as last year.

'It's no use, Alfie,' groaned Fitzer, throwing the spanner back into his dad's toolbox. 'It's wrecked from the crash.'

'I know,' Alfie said. 'There's no way it will be fixed for tomorrow.'

There were only three teams in this year's junior race – The Hot Rod Squad, Whacker's Wheelies and The Green Machine.

The other teams had pulled out because of Whacker Walsh. Whacker had caused the crash last year that wrecked Alfie's go-kart.

The Hot Rod Squad, with Roddy Cooper and his sister, Becky, were favourites to win. Their dad owned a garage and he helped make their kart the fastest in Budsville.

'We should have tried to get a different go-kart,' suggested Fitzer, 'this one is too old.'

'No way!' Alfie said. 'This was my grandad's go-kart. It won lots of races.'

'But Alfie, it's a heap of junk!' giggled Fitzer.

Alfie took a long look at The Green Machine. Fitzer was right. Sadly he wheeled the old go-kart around to the back garden. They would have to pull out of the race.

CHAPTER 2

GREEN SAND!

That night, Alfie couldn't sleep. He kept thinking about the race, and the go-kart, and his grandad. Maybe, if he **really, really** tried, he could still fix The Green Machine in time.

As soon as he saw the first light in the sky, he hopped out of bed and ran down to the garden.

'**JEEPERS CREEPERS!**' he yelled. The garden, the path, all the rooftops were covered in sparkling green sand.

Alfie wiped some sand off a holly bush and felt his hand tingle.

'Thanks, Alfie,' said the holly. 'That was making my leaves itchy.'

'Where did it come from?' Alfie asked.

'A big wind blew in last night and this stuff just fell from the sky,' the holly replied. 'I've never seen anything like it.'

Suddenly Alfie heard someone laughing. Who could be up at this hour? He ran around to the front garden and saw Mrs Butler dancing in

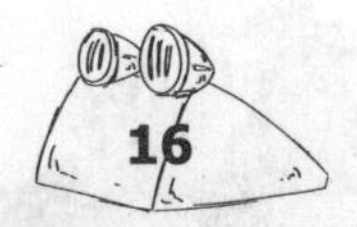

the street. She was twirling round and round in the sparkling sand – in her bare feet!

'Are you okay, Mrs Butler?' Alfie asked.

'I'm **WONDERFUL**, Alfie,' Mrs Butler sang, and cartwheeled over the wall into her garden.

There must be magic in this sand, Alfie thought. And who knew all about magic? The wise old plant, of course.

Alfie lifted the loose floorboard in the shed and took out the old box.

He opened the magical book and put his hand on the first page.

Up rose the wise old plant, unfolding its crinkly leaves until it towered above Alfie.

'You're up early, Alfie,' yawned the plant. 'What's your problem?'

'Sand,' said Alfie.

'Sand?' repeated the plant. 'Do you need sand?'

'No! Sand **is** the problem. It's green and sparkly, and it's **EVERYWHERE**.'

'Sparkling green sand?' The wise old plant looked very worried. 'Show me.'

Alfie ran out and came back with a handful of the strange sand.

'Oh dear, I was afraid of that,' the plant shook his head in horror.

'What's wrong?' Alfie asked.

'This sand is not from your world, Alfie. It's from the Desert of Doom, on the very edge of Arcania.'

CHAPTER 3

The Emerald Cactus

The wise old plant pointed to a page in the magical book.

Alfie looked in and saw a huge sandstorm blowing up from the desert.

'What's happening?' he asked.

'A very long time ago, Alfie, the Fortune Palms gave your grandfather a warning: one day the four great winds of Arcania would come together over the Desert of Doom and crash into the sands. The Emerald Cactus

would explode into millions of pieces and be carried away in the sandstorm.'

'So that's why the sand is green,' Alfie said, nodding. 'But what is the Emerald Cactus, and why did it blow here?'

'The Emerald Cactus is a plant with great powers,' explained the wise old plant. 'Powers that can be used for good or evil. The Fortune Palms told your grandad that after the explosion the Cactus would seek the help of the Keeper of the Crystal Orchid.'

'But that's me!' Alfie exclaimed.

'Yes, Alfie,' said the plant. 'You are the Keeper. That's why the sand is here. The Keeper is the only one who can help the Emerald Cactus now.'

'What can I do?'

'First you have to collect every bit of green sand in Budsville. Then you must return the sand to the Desert of Doom and shine the crystal orchid on it. The powers of the two great forces will join and the sand will turn back into the Emerald Cactus.'

'Wow!' gasped Alfie. 'That's going to take me FOREVER!'

'Maybe not. Stand back, Alfie,' warned the wise old plant.

He pointed his crinkly leaves at a crack in the floorboards.

Suddenly the floor began to

shudder. A bright blue light shone through the crack and a big hole opened up in the middle of the floor. When the light dimmed, Alfie saw a narrow staircase going right down underneath the shed.

CHAPTER 4

THE SECRET SUBWAY

Alfie nearly fell down the stairs in amazement.

'A stairs in the shed! Where does it go?'

'This staircase,' said the wise old plant, 'will bring you to the secret Supersonic Subway.'

'The secret **Superwhatsit**??? Where did that come from?'

'Your grandad made it, Alfie,'

smiled the wise old plant.

Alfie was shocked. 'Grandad built a subway? No way!'

The wise old plant laughed out loud.

'Not all by himself, Alfie. He was helped by a colony of Arcanian Ants that he rescued from an ant-eating troll.'

Alfie began to walk down the stairs. 'Where does the subway lead?' he called back to the wise old plant.

'Hold on.' The plant *s-t-r-e-t-c-h-e-d* and dipped his head over the staircase.

'To the left,' he said, pointing, 'the subway goes under the streets of Budsville. To the right it goes under Arcania and comes out at the Desert of Doom.'

'Wow!' said Alfie. 'There must have been *billions* of ants.'

'Not really,' laughed the plant, 'Arcanian Ants are MUCH bigger than Budsville ants.'

There was another surprise for
Alfie at the bottom of the stairs.

'Crikey! That looks like the broken lawnmower Grandad threw out years ago. But what's happened to it? Look at all the knobs and buttons and levers!'

'Well,' explained the wise old plant, 'your grandad and I had to make some changes so the mower would be ready.'

'Ready for what?' Alfie asked.

'Listen carefully,' said the wise old plant. 'First, this machine will help you collect the green sand. Then you will have to face the evil Desert Elves.'

Alfie didn't like the sound of that.

'What have evil elves got to do with it?'

'The Desert Elves have being trying for all of Arcanian time to capture the Emerald Cactus and use its powers for evil. And now is their chance.'

'Are you telling me that these Desert Elves are coming to Budsville?' Alfie asked.

'Yes, Alfie,' replied the wise old plant.

'But if they are elves, won't it take them a long time?'

'Not **these** elves. They travel on the wind on chariots drawn by Giant Scorpions.'

'So, when **are** they coming?'

The wise old plant looked sadly at Alfie. 'They are already on their way!'

'So, there's no time to lose,' added the plant. 'Here's what you must do. Under the seat of the mower you will find instructions that your grandad left. Read them carefully.'

Alfie reached down and pulled out a folded sheet of paper.

'Now – and this is very important – you must wear these special goggles.'

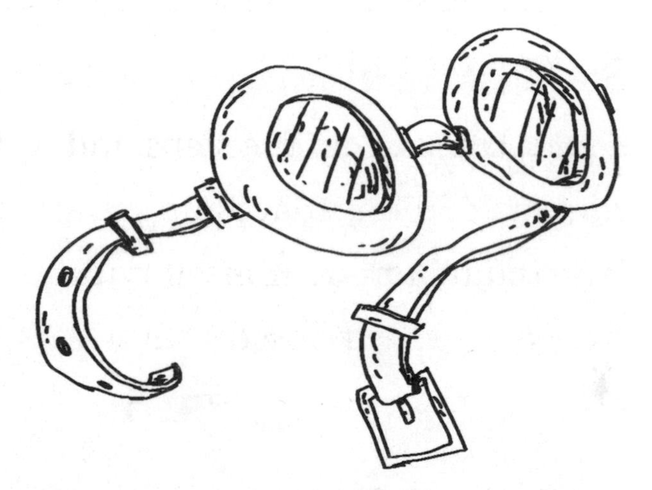

Alfie looked at the thick rubber goggles with the rainbow-coloured glass. 'Why do I have to wear them?'

'Desert Elves are INVISIBLE,' said the wise old plant. 'Without these

goggles you won't be able to see them. Oh, and don't forget your crystal orchid,' he said, as he wound his way back up the stairs.

As Alfie ran up the steps and pocketed the crystal orchid, he saw the wise old plant fold himself back into the book, which closed with a

CHAPTER 5

VVRROOOOM!

Alfie jumped onto the magic mower. Following Grandad's instructions, he pressed the starting button.

VVRROOOOM, VVRROOOOM – the engine sounded more like a space rocket than a lawnmower.

Then it flashed with green, red and blue lights, and two dazzling headlights shone out of the front.

Alfie turned the wheel to the left and pushed the **GO** button.

Zoooooooom! Alfie and the super mower raced through the Supersonic Subway. Under the streets of Budsville it spun around corners, dipped down, and shot up again.

It was like the best rollercoaster ever!

Suddenly a red light blinked on the front panel.

EXIT! EXIT!
EXIT! EXIT!

The word flashed on and off, on and off.

Before Alfie had a chance to do anything, the magic mower headed straight up towards an iron manhole cover. They were going to be

FLATTENED

At the very last second, Alfie found the **EXIT** button. **THUMP!** A red boxing glove on springs shot out of the front of the machine and **PUNCHED** the manhole out of the way.

The machine shot through the hole. Alfie slammed on the brakes and the machine skidded to a halt through a pile of sparkling green sand on the street.

Phew! Alfie thought, that was scary. He looked around. Good! Everybody was still in bed, so nobody had seen the sand except Mrs Butler.

Right! I better get on with this.

He pressed the button that said **VACUUM** and a big pipe slid out from the back of the machine. There was a huge **S-U-C-K-I-N-G** noise. Slowly the

green sand began to move towards the machine. Faster and faster it came. From gardens and cars and rooftops it raced up the pipe and into the mower.

All of it! Every last bit. Not one grain of sand was left. How could so much sand fit inside the machine?

Now for the Desert Elves, Alfie thought. He snapped the special goggles back on and looked around. There was no sign of them yet. Maybe they wouldn't come at all?

CHAPTER 6

THE GREEN MACHINE 2

Fitzer opened his bedroom window and looked out. His jaw dropped as he spotted Alfie Green sitting on the weirdest, maddest-looking lawnmower he had ever seen.

Fitzer raced across the street in his pyjamas.

'Alfie, what's that thing you're on?'

'Eh ... em ... um ...,' Alfie stuttered. 'It's ... it's ... oh, yeah, it's The Green Machine 2.'

'Wow! Alfie, it's deadly,' Fitzer gasped. 'Listen, I've got to get dressed. See you later for the race.'

Oops, thought Alfie. Shouldn't have said that. He moved the machine out of the street and behind a hedge. Then he waited. And waited. And waited.

'There you are, Alfie.' Fitzer's head popped up over the hedge. 'I thought you were lost. It's race time. Let's go.'

Poor Alfie. Everyone laughed at his machine.

'Hey, Alfie!' yelled Whacker Walsh. 'Love the trendy goggles.'

'Yeah! They match your trendy lawnmower,' laughed Hot Roddy Cooper.

Alfie was furious. 'I'm out of here, Fitzer!'

'What! Are you crazy?' replied Fitzer. 'Don't mind those idiots. You'll SKIN them.'

They settled into their karts.

'Let the race begin,' called Mr Skully, raising the flag above his head.

Whacker Walsh revved his engine.

Hot Roddy Cooper revved his engine even louder.

Alfie didn't rev his engine at all.

'One. Two. Three.' Mr Skully dropped the flag.

Hot Roddy blasted off into the lead, closely followed by Whacker Walsh.

Alfie didn't even move. He just sat there looking around him. Where are those elves, he wondered?

Fitzer ran over to Alfie.

'Alfie, what's wrong? Get going.'

Just then, Alfie's engine revved up.

'Out of the way, Fitzer,' Alfie warned.

'YES!' cheered Fitzer. 'You can do it, Alfie. You can win!'

CHAPTER 7

DESERT ELVES

Alfie didn't care about winning. He had just seen two Scorpion Chariots racing through the sky towards him. Riding on each chariot were two nasty-looking creatures dressed in dusty red armour made from scorpion shells.

They had oval eyes and pointy ears that stuck out of their stinger helmets. Two jagged teeth hung from their black lips.

'Get the
boy,'
screeched one
of the Desert
Elves, unleashing a
terrifying crack of his
cactus whip.

'Time to go,' yelled Alfie and he blasted off down the road.

Whacker Walsh couldn't believe his eyes as The Green Machine 2 sped past him around Laurel Park.

Alfie could see the Scorpion Chariots with his special goggles, but poor Whacker couldn't. The chariots roared past Whacker.

One of the Desert Elves cracked his whip at Whacker's go-kart and lifted it up in the air.

'Hey! Whacker's go-kart can fly! That's cheating,' shouted Fitzer.

'Aaaaaagh!' screamed Whacker as he crash-landed in the duck pond.

The Desert Elves were catching up on Alfie. He increased his speed and raced past Hot Roddy Cooper, leaving

him choking on lawnmower fumes.

Hot Roddy stamped on his accelerator as hard as he could, but couldn't get near Alfie.

Everybody cheered, especially Fitzer, as The Green Machine 2 **rocketed** past the finish line, with Hot Roddy way behind in second place.

'Stop, Alfie! It's over. You've won!'

Fitzer ran down the road, but couldn't see Alfie anywhere.

HOT ROD

CHAPTER 8

Down! Down!

The Scorpion Chariots were just behind Alfie as he ducked down the open manhole.

'Down! Down!' screeched the Desert Elves. The chariots chased The Green Machine 2 through the twisting, turning Supersonic Subway under Budsville.

Pictures fell from walls, cups fell off tables and Old Podge's prize carrots popped right up out of the ground as

The Green Machine 2 thundered under the houses.

Mrs Butler got such a fright that she ran out of her house screaming, 'It's an earthquake'. And she forgot all about the strange green sand she had seen that morning.

Alfie raced ahead until finally he could see beneath his garden shed. Just as his grandad had instructed, he slowed down.

The Desert Elves cracked their whips and charged towards Alfie.

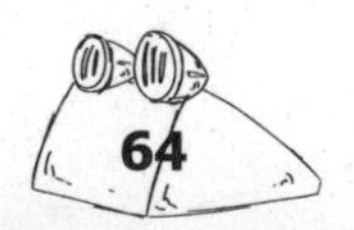

Thanks to Grandad, Alfie was ready for them.

He pulled the RELEASE lever. A huge net spun out and trapped the Scorpion Chariots.

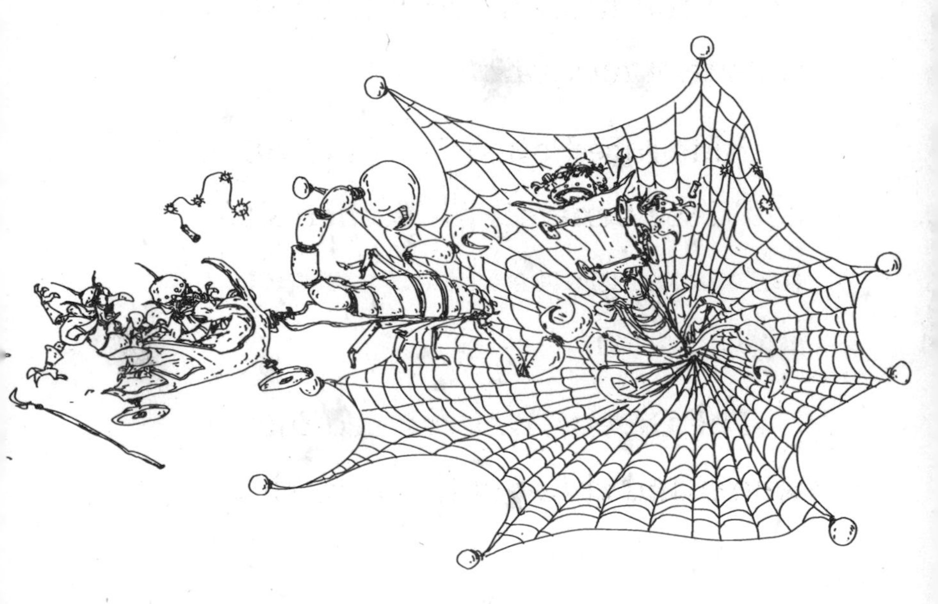

Then Alfie swung the steering wheel to the right and pressed the SUPERSONIC button.

ZOOOOOOOOM! The Green Machine tore off at supersonic speed through the subway under Arcania, towing the chariots and the struggling Desert Elves behind.

Within seconds, it BLASTED up through the sands of the Desert of Doom.

Then Alfie did the most important thing of all – he HIT THE BRAKES.

SWOOOOOOSH! The Scorpion

Chariots and their passengers were flung through the air. They got smaller and smaller, until they disappeared way beyond the Desert of Doom.

Alfie sat for a while, trying to catch his breath. Then he pressed the button marked EMPTY. Showers of sparkling green sand flew out from The Green Machine and rested in a huge mound.

Only one thing left to do, Alfie thought, taking the Crystal Orchid out of his pocket.

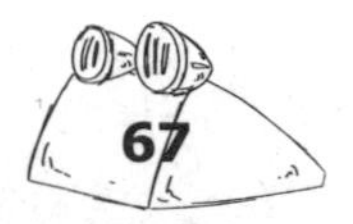

He grasped the orchid tightly and pointed it at the green sand.

With a blinding flash of light the Emerald Cactus rose up from the desert sands and Alfie and The Green Machine 2 found themselves back beneath the shed.

CHAPTER 9

WHAT'S YOUR SECRET?

Alfie switched off the mower and ran back upstairs.

As soon as his foot lifted off the last step, the stairs folded up and became the floor of the shed once more.

He put the crystal orchid back in its biscuit tin, and the magical book under the floorboard before locking the shed door behind him.

'Hey! There's Alfie,' yelled Fitzer and he ran up Budsville Avenue,

followed by a shocked Hot Roddy Cooper and a drenched Whacker Walsh.

‘Nice one, Alfie,’ congratulated Fitzer.

‘Where’s your mad lawnmower gone?’ Hot Roddy asked.

‘Yeah!’ added Whacker, pulling strands of pond slime off his head. ‘How did that banger of yours go so fast?’

‘What’s your secret, Alfie?’ Hot Roddy wanted to know.

Alfie smiled at Roddy and Whacker, put his arm around Fitzer and answered, ‘Let’s just say, I imagined that I was being chased by

Giant Scorpion-drawn Chariots with Evil Elves on board. Wouldn't that make anything move at supersonic speed?'

Then Alfie and Fitzer danced their way down Budsville Avenue, singing, 'You'll never beat The Green Machine.'

READ ALFIE'S OTHER GREAT ADVENTURES IN:

CHECK OUT ALL OUR CHILDREN'S BOOKS ON

PRAISE FOR THE

ALFIE GREEN SERIES

'Gorgeous books, beautifully illustrated.'

Sunday Independent

'A great choice for boys and girls.'

Irish Independent

'Bright, breezy and full of flesh crawling incidents. Young readers will love this.'

Village

'Best writer ever.' Siobhan Quigley (age 8)

Laois Voice

'*Alfie Green and the Magical Gift* was the best book I have ever read in my life.' Hannah Meaney (age 7)

Clare People

Belching Bogs
Valley
Skeleton
Woods
The Crooked
Firethorn
The Swamp
Honeycomb
Mountain
Sleepy Meadows
Nanabur
Mines
SUPERSONIC SUBWAY
Alfie's
House
BUDSVILLE AVENUE